a work of fiction in 34 ½ chapters
(with some non-fiction mixed in free of charge) by

MICHAEL ROSEN

UNCLE GOBB
AND THE DREAD SHED

with important pictures full of interest,
terror and toast by

NEAL LAYTON

BLOOMSBURY
LONDON NEW DELHI NEW YORK SYDNEY

Bloomsbury Publishing, London, New Delhi, New York and Sydney

First published in Great Britain in June 2015 by Bloomsbury Publishing Plc
50 Bedford Square, London WC1B 3DP

www.bloomsbury.com

Bloomsbury is a registered trademark of Bloomsbury Publishing Plc

Text copyright © Michael Rosen 2015
Illustrations copyright © Neal Layton 2015

The moral rights of the author and illustrator have been asserted

A CIP catalogue record for this book is available from the British Library

ISBN 978 1 4088 5130 2

FSC
www.fsc.org
MIX
Paper from
responsible sources
FSC® C020471

Printed and bound in Great Britain
by CPI Group (UK) Ltd, Croydon CR0 4YY

1 3 5 7 9 10 8 6 4 2

For Emma, Elsie and Emile

CHAPTER 1

Amazing Things Going On With His Face

It all began when Malcolm looked through the keyhole. Of course he shouldn't have looked. Well, there shouldn't really have been a keyhole.

I mean, why was there a keyhole on the bathroom door anyway? What did the keyhole think it was doing sitting there stuck on a bathroom door?

That's a very good point.

So really it was the keyhole's fault.

This is what happened:

Uncle Gobb came to stay. No one liked Uncle Gobb.

More on him in a minute.

Uncle Gobb went to the bathroom.

Not the American kind of bathroom which is also a restroom. This can be confusing. Are you supposed to rest in the bath? But they don't mean the bath anyway. When they say 'bathroom', they mean the room where you go to pee and poo. Unless they mean you're supposed to pee and poo in the bath. Which they don't.

So there was no need to bring that up.
Sorry.

NOT
THIS

Let's get on.

Uncle Gobb went to the bathroom. That's the kind of bathroom which has a bath in it. And a sink. He was standing at the sink, looking in the mirror. People often do that. They look in the mirror and talk to themselves. They say things like,

'Hiya, handsome, you're looking good today.'

Or,

'What's cooking?'

Or,

'I've got a little green bit on my chin … I wonder if I'm going mouldy…'

Uncle Gobb wasn't saying any of these things.

He was polishing his face.

Now, everyone knew that Uncle Gobb had a shiny face. And just to be clear, it's perfectly OK for people to have shiny faces. And it's perfectly OK for people to shine their shiny faces. The thing is, Malcolm had never ever seen anyone shine their face before.

This is what happened:

Malcolm was crouching down looking through the keyhole. He saw Uncle Gobb take a piece of cloth in his right hand; in his left hand he took some stuff to make windows shiny. He squirted the shiny stuff into the cloth, took the cloth up to his face and started shining. Round and round and round, over his cheeks, his chin, his forehead till it was all very, very shiny.

When he had finished, Uncle Gobb looked in the mirror and said, 'Hey, Gobby, you're looking good today.'

Malcolm stared. Well, it was one-eye staring because the keyhole wasn't big enough for him to do a full two-eye stare.

In fact, he was wondering whether one-eye staring could be a new kind of competition at the Olympics when the door opened and there was Uncle Gobb. He looked down at Malcolm, who was now trying very hard to stop one-eye staring, and said, 'That doesn't look like homework to me.'

Ah, you might be wondering why Uncle Gobb would say such a thing. Of course someone kneeling on the floor outside a bathroom doing one-eye staring through a keyhole doesn't look like homework. What an obvious and silly thing to say. But why did Uncle Gobb say such an obvious and silly thing?

To find out the answer to this and to why tomatoes are red, we will need to press on to the next chapter, which is chapter 2.

CHAPTER 2

Why Uncle Gobb Said, 'That Doesn't Look Like Homework To Me.'

You'll see that this chapter is not called:

'Why Uncle Gobb Said, "That Doesn't Look Like Homework to Me" AND Why Tomatoes Are Red.'

I'm sorry, we may never find out in this book why tomatoes are red. There are other kinds of book which explain things like that. They're called '**non-fiction books**' and they're very good too. My favourite is one called *Don't Eat Your Best Friend.*

CHAPTER 2 AND A 1/2

Some Explanation And A BLAMMM!!!

Wherever Malcolm went in life, he thought that people would ask him why he lived with Uncle Gobb. This was the explanation he had ready:

'Many years ago, Uncle Gobb was married to someone called Tammy. Things didn't work out between Uncle Gobb and Tammy, because when they got together, it made a terrible mixture which exploded.

'They picked themselves up and said, "We've made a bit of a mess – best not do that again, huh?"'

'Uncle Gobb and Tammy didn't stay married after that.

'Now Uncle Gobb has nowhere to live (the

blew their house up) so he came to live with me and my mum.'

I can tell you that this is as near to the truth as it is possible to be.

CHAPTER 3

The Real Chapter, On Why Uncle Gobb Said, 'That Doesn't Look Like Homework To Me.'

Uncle Gobb was very keen on homework. He liked talking to people about homework. His sister was called Tess and Tess was Malcolm's mum.

This is what happened next:

'Tess,' Uncle Gobb said, 'the boy needs to do more homework.'

'Tess,' he said, 'the dog needs to do more homework.'

'Tess,' he said, 'the table needs to do more homework.'

Yes, as far as Uncle Gobb was concerned, everyone and everything needed to do more homework.

'Tess,' he said, 'if they don't do more homework, we'll fall behind and we'll all be ruined.'

When he said that, the dog got up, walked slowly over to Uncle Gobb and bit his leg.

I can tell you that that was the last time Uncle Gobb ever said that the dog needed to do more homework.

I can also tell you that the table didn't get up and bite Uncle Gobb's leg. It had legs of its own to worry about. Four of them actually.

(That was a **non-fiction FACT** for you to make up for the fact that I haven't told you why tomatoes are red. I figured that you were rather sad and angry that I didn't tell you about the tomatoes and now you're feeling a bit happier that I've told you the thing about tables. I hope so.)

When Uncle Gobb said, 'The boy needs to do more homework', the 'boy' he was talking about was of course Malcolm. So Malcolm said to Uncle Gobb, 'Well you don't do any homework, Uncle Gobb, so why should I have to?'

At that, Uncle Gobb pulled himself up to his full height and said, 'Aha, my boy, but how do you think I got so far in life if it wasn't for the fact that I did my homework?'

This is what is known as the

KILLER ANSWER!

This is not an answer that kills. That would be terrible. Imagine being asked a question like, 'What's the time?' And you say, 'Half past three.' And the moment you said it, the person who asked you the time dropped down dead.

That would be awful. And shouldn't be even thought about. So stop thinking about it.

Thank you.

No, the Killer Answer is the answer that leaves the person who asked the question with nothing else to say. Not even an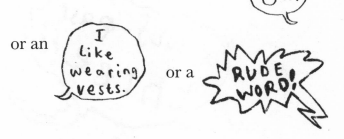

(You'll notice there that I didn't write the rude word. I just wrote 'rude word' which you're allowed to do in books like this when you can't write the rude word itself.)

So Uncle Gobb delivered the Killer Answer. 'How do you think I got so far in life if it wasn't for the fact that I did my homework?'

Malcolm couldn't think of anything to say. Nothing at all. Well, for about three seconds, he couldn't.

CHAPTER 4

Three Seconds Later

'Uncle Gobb,' said Malcolm, 'just how far have you got in life?'

For some reason this made Uncle Gobb very, very angry.

He stared at Malcolm and said,

'LISTEN HERE, YOU **DISRESPECTFUL LITTLE WEASEL**. I AM AN IMPORTANT PERSON. I HAVE BEEN AN IMPORTANT PERSON FOR MANY YEARS. YOU MAY NOT KNOW IT BUT OUT THERE AND OVER THERE AND ROUND THERE AND IN AND OUT THE ARCHES, I AM LOOKED UP TO. PEOPLE PASS ME IN THE STREET AND SAY, "THERE GOES UNCLE GOBB." WHEN I SAY, "TEA!" PEOPLE BRING ME TEA.

WHEN I SAY, "COAT!" PEOPLE BRING ME MY COAT. SO LISTEN HERE, YOU DISRESPECTFUL LITTLE WEASEL, WHEN I SAY, "YOU NEED TO DO MORE HOMEWORK", YOU SHOULD DO MORE HOMEWORK. AND IF YOU DON'T DO MORE HOMEWORK, YOU'LL BE PUT IN THE DREAD SHED.'

'THE **DREAD SHED**?'
said Malcolm.

'YES – THE **DREAD SHED**!'
said Uncle Gobb.

Tess looked up.

'Oh come off it, Derek, you do go on, don't you? Why don't you nip out to the shops and get some milk. We're running low.'

Malcolm looked at Mum. Malcolm looked at Uncle Gobb.

They really were very different. Not just because Mum was a woman and Uncle Gobb was a man. (A bit more **non-fiction** for you there.) They were different in just about everything. Including that polishing-face thing.

Mum didn't polish her face. She did put some other stuff on her face but she didn't shine it up with a cloth.

Malcolm liked that.

And they were different in the way they talked. The words they used.

Malcolm thought about that and started to wonder about the word 'disrespectful'. What did it mean? And are weasels disrespectful?

weasels
being
WEASELLY

MEASELS

CHAPTER 5

Weasels

Weasels shouldn't be confused with measles, easels or teasels.

Measles is the name of a very unpleasant illness.

Easels are things that artists use to put things on which they then cover with paint.

Teasels are a kind of thistle.

Weasels aren't measles.

Weasels aren't easels.

Weasels aren't teasels.

Weasels are weaselly little animals who

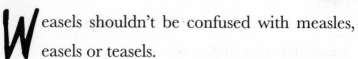

WEASEL = TEASEL
WEASEL = MEASLE
WEASEL = EASEL
WEASEL

WE~~ASEL~~ = TEASEL

WE~~ASEL~~ = MEASLE

~~WEASEL~~ = EASEL

~~WEASEL~~ =

run about being weaselly.

On television, on the radio, and in newspapers you might hear someone say the expression 'weasel words'. 'Weasel words' are when you say things to help you wriggle out of admitting you did something wrong. Like, 'I didn't punch him – he ran very fast towards my fist.'

This is one of the strangest things you'll ever hear anyone say in the whole of your life for the simple reason that weasels don't talk. They don't use words. That's not what weasels do.

If ever you're with anyone and they say, 'Weasel words', you could point that out to them. Don't do it in a sneery, smarty-pants sort

MORE weasels ← being WEASELLY

of a way. Just say it gently and nicely as you would if you were talking to a weasel. 'Excuse me,' you say, 'but weasels don't use words.'

Anyway, now you know all about weasels.

CHAPTER 6

The Milk

'Before you go to get the milk, Uncle Gobb,' Malcolm said, 'are weasels disrespectful?'

Uncle Gobb went off to get the milk.

CHAPTER 7

The Milk. Again.

Uncle Gobb was gone for some time.

When he walked back in, he said, 'Tess, I want you to make clear to the boy that I am an important person. I am someone who is in charge.'

Mum looked up.

'Yes, yes, Derek, but you've forgotten to get the milk.'

CHAPTER 8

And What Is The Dread Shed?

Just in case you're wondering why I've asked that question, that's because after Uncle Gobb said that Malcolm was a disrespectful little weasel, you'll remember that he said that he would put Malcolm in the **DREAD SHED**.

So, now we're asking: What is the …

A long time ago, when the world was nothing more than a primeval soup of hydrogen, oxygen, nitrogen and tomato ketchup, there was a builder called Dave...

Oh hang on, it must have been after the primeval-soup-bit of history. I'll do that again.

A long time ago when street lamps were lit by gas and chimneys poured out smoke from

the chimney stacks, a woman by the name of Elizabeth Fear went to the Prime Minister and said, 'Prime Minister, there are some bad children out there.'

'I know,' said the Prime Minister, 'I was bad once. I climbed into my father's Rolls Royce

Super Silver Bullet Cloud and drove round his parklands terrifying the deer. I was only twelve.'

'No, no, no,' said Elizabeth Fear, 'not rich and bad. I mean poor and bad. They're the ones we have to deal with.'

'Oh, very well,' said the Prime Minister, very relieved that this fierce Elizabeth Fear

wasn't going to punish him for that driving-round-the-parklands crime.

'I suggest,' said Elizabeth, 'that in every area of the country, we build special cabins, and whenever there are poor bad children we shove them in there. And they shall be called "**DREAD SHEDS**",' she cried out.

'**DREAD SHEDS**, I like the sound of that,' said the Prime Minister. 'There's a whole rhyming chiming bizz going on there. "**DREAD SHED**", she said. She said, "**DREAD SHED**". "The Shed's Dread", she said.'

'Can I take that as a "Yes"?' said Elizabeth Fear.

'Take that as a "Yes",' said the Prime Minister.

And that is the story of how **DREAD SHEDS** came about.

But – and here's an interesting thing:
DREAD SHEDS were abolished, banned, stopped, ceased, terminated, finished.

There were no more **DREAD SHEDS** left.

What happened was this:

(Shall we have a new chapter for this? Yes, let's.)

CHAPTER 9

No More Dread Sheds

A long time ago when the Beatles sang nicely and everyone was happy, the Prime Minister (a different Prime Minister) said, 'I don't think locking up poor children in sheds is a very nice thing to do. No more **DREAD SHEDS**.'

And there weren't.

Uncle Gobb's father, who was called Father Gobb, was furious.

'That's where all the trouble started!' he shouted at little Uncle Gobb, who wasn't Uncle Gobb at the time, he was little Derek Gobb and his sister was (as we know) Tess Gobb.

'When some stupid fat-head abolished **DREAD SHEDS**, that was the end of everything. Children stopped respecting their mothers and fathers, teenage boys became teenagers, and people started doing bad things.'

Tess said, 'Father Gobb, teenage boys would be teenagers because ... er ... they were teenagers.'

At this, Father Gobb became even more furious. 'I say the River Tiber will run with blood,' he shouted at Tess, the thunder flying out of his nostrils. What he actually meant was that a whole lot of awful stuff will happen. Even dying. This was a strange thing for him to say because the River Tiber is in Ponky.

Sorry, I mean, the River Tiber is in Rome.

(The reason why I made that mistake – calling Rome 'Ponky' – will be explained later. Please don't expect everything to be in the right order in this book.)

So little Derek Gobb, who always wanted to please Father Gobb, made a special vow, a special promise.

For his father's sake, he would save a **DREAD SHED**. If that silly Prime Minister thought he could get rid of all the **DREAD SHEDS**, he was wrong. He, little Derek Gobb, would save one.

So, that night when all was dark, and cats prowled the streets looking for open bedroom windows so that they could hang about outside making a howling noise, little Derek Gobb scurried through the shadows lit by the whites of his own eyes. He was heading for the nearest **DREAD SHED**.

In his pocket were 127 very small wheels called 'castors' which he had stolen off the bottoms of armchairs and sofas at the nearest

Department Store, called 'Ramsays, your local Department Store'.

He approached the **DREAD SHED**, which sat menacingly in a dell next to the gasworks.

Fearlessly, he stuck all 127 castors under the edges and corners of the **DREAD SHED** and then silently, slowly, carefully and secretly, using the old rope (for which he had paid money, as in 'money for old rope'), he pulled the **DREAD SHED** through the cat-prowly-howly streets all the way home. Then cunningly, cleverly, wisely and coolly he nudged the **DREAD SHED** into the back yard of their family home.

Then he wrote a note:

Dear Father,

When you get up and come downstairs, you will see a large shed-like building in our back yard. It is a **Dread Shed**, which I have captured, for, Father, I have listened to your words of wisdom and acted upon them. This **Dread Shed** will keep alive forever the glory that is the **Dread Shed** and when the time comes, just as one day King Arthur will rise from the cave wherein he sleeps to save our kingdom, so our **Dread Shed** will arise and save our kingdom too.

Love,

(or something like it, in case that sounds too soppy)

Derek.

And little Derek Gobb dropped this note on the pillow beside Father Gobb's head even as he lay sleeping.

That's why in the morning, Father Gobb did NOT wake up, go downstairs and say, 'What the blooming hell is that shed doing in our back yard?'

Instead, he looked longingly and lovingly at the **DREAD SHED** and slapped Derek round the top of his head because that was the only way Father Gobb knew how to say thank you to his children.

And now, little Derek Gobb had grown up. He had become Uncle Gobb, and the **DREAD SHED** had stayed with him in his

life. It didn't blow up in the

It lurked in a corner of the back yard.

CHAPTER 10

The Next Day: Something Strange At School

Malcolm and his great, greatest, best, bestest, most wonderfullest best-best-best friend Crackersnacker were sitting in class doing a worksheet.

In case you don't know what a worksheet is, it's one of those sheets of paper where there are bits of writing followed by gaps. You read the bits of writing and then you write something in the gaps.

This is why you go to school. You go to school to fill in the gaps.

In recent years, worksheets have been made much more exciting by moving them on to computers, tablets, iPhones and iScreams. They're exactly the same questions, exactly the same answers, but instead of writing them, you tap in the numbers or the letters of the words from a keypad.

HURRAH!!!

THE HISTORY OF WORKSHEETS - A NON-FICTION SECTION

WORKSHEETS WERE INVENTED BY JEREMIAH WORKSHEET IN 1859. BEFORE HE INVENTED WORKSHEETS, HE INVENTED TROUSERS. SADLY, HE DISCOVERED THAT SOMEONE HAD INVENTED TROUSERS BEFORE HIM, SO NO ONE WAS INTERESTED IN THE JEREMIAH WORKSHEET TROUSERS.

HOWEVER, THE DAY HE INVENTED A PIECE OF PAPER WITH WRITING AND GAPS ON IT, WAS THE DAY HE **CHANGED THE WORLD**.

SOON, HIS PIECES OF PAPER WITH WRITING AND GAPS ON IT WERE TURNING UP IN SCHOOLS ALL OVER THE COUNTRY, THEN EUROPE, THEN THE NORTHERN HEMISPHERE, THE SOUTHERN HEMISPHERE, THE WESTERN HEMISPHERE, THE EASTERN HEMISPHERE, THE NORTH-WESTERN HEMISPHERE, THE SOUTH-EASTERN HEMISPHERE, THE-
(HEY, HANG ON, HOW MANY HEMISPHERES HAS THIS SPHERE GOT?)
- UNTIL THEY WERE IN SCHOOLS ALL OVER THE WORLD.

AT THE BOTTOM OF ALL THE FIRST EXAMPLES OF THESE PIECES OF PAPER WITH WRITING AND GAPS ON THEM WERE THE WORDS 'JEREMIAH WORKSHEET' BUT ONE DAY, A PRINTER IN LAMBETH IN LONDON LEFT THE WORD 'JEREMIAH' OFF THE PIECES OF PAPER WITH WRITING AND GAPS ON THEM SO THAT ALL IT SAID WAS 'WORKSHEET'.

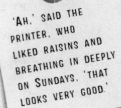

'AH,' SAID THE PRINTER, WHO LIKED RAISINS AND BREATHING IN DEEPLY ON SUNDAYS, 'THAT LOOKS VERY GOOD.'

SOON ALL THE PRINTERS — EVEN THE ONES WHO DIDN'T LIKE RAISINS AND BREATHING IN DEEPLY ON SUNDAYS — THOUGHT THAT THE PIECES OF PAPER WITH WRITING AND GAPS ON, LOOKED BEST WITH JUST 'WORKSHEET' WRITTEN ON THEM.

AND THAT'S HOW WORKSHEETS CAME TO BE CALLED 'WORKSHEETS'.

END OF THE HISTORY OF WORKSHEETS AND THE NON-FICTION SECTION

So, Malcolm and his great friend Crackersnacker were doing a worksheet.

A word or two about Crackersnacker, who I think you'll quite like:

Crackersnacker was one of those boys they used to describe as 'peaky'. Do you know what 'peaky' means? Well, a long time ago, there used to be factories, mills and chimneys where boys and girls had to go and work. All boys and girls who worked in factories, mills and chimneys were peaky.

Crackersnacker didn't work in a factory, mill or chimney but somehow or another, he still managed to look peaky.

CHAPTER 11

A Quick But Important Scene With Malcolm And Crackersnacker In Which They Discuss Uncle Gobb

Crackersnacker: You know that geezer who lives with you and your mum?

Malcolm: Yep.

Crackersnacker: Is he your mum's boyfriend?

Malcolm: Nope.

Crackersnacker: Who is he then?

Malcolm: He's my uncle.

Crackersnacker: What's he like?

Malcolm: He always wants me to do more homework and I end up being bamboozled and confuzled. I can't stand it.

Crackersnacker: Oh yeah?

Malcolm: Yeah, and if I don't do the homework, he says he'll put me in the **DREAD SHED**.

Crackersnacker: What's a **DREAD SHED**?

Malcolm: Well, a long time ago, when streets were lit by gas…

Crackersnacker: What?

Malcolm: Oh, never mind. I'll tell you another time. What's important is that I must get him to move out.

Crackersnacker: Right. Do you like dark chocolate or milk chocolate?

Malcolm: Milk chocolate.

Crackersnacker: Me too.

CHAPTER 12

The Worksheet – Continued

The worksheet said:

'Billy was wearing a blue hat.'

Then it said:

'What colour was Billy's hat?'

Malcolm stared at the piece of writing. He looked for a clue to the answer. Was there anything to help him answer the question? Nope.

This sort of thing made Malcolm worried
and sad.

'Psst, Crackersnacker. What's the answer?'
Malcolm said in a pssst sort of a voice.

'Blue,' said Crackersnacker.

'I'm not so sure about that,' said Malcolm.
So he wrote underneath

I don't know.

Now just at that moment, his teacher, Mr Keenly, was walking past.

'Well, well, well,' said Mr Keenly in a kind voice, 'let's see if I can help: Billy was wearing a BLUE hat. What colour was his hat?'

When Mr Keenly said the word 'blue' he opened his eyes wide, pushed his mouth forwards in a keenly sort of a way, and made his finger draw a wiggly underliney sort of a line.

Malcolm had often noticed that Mr Keenly had this interesting way of explaining things. If you didn't get what he was telling you, or if you didn't understand what was on a worksheet, he would just say it again but with loads of eye-opening, mouth-moving, finger-wiggling things.

This meant that Malcolm just said what he had said again too.

'I don't know, sir.'

Mr Keenly frowned. 'Billy's hat is blue, Malcolm.'

Malcolm looked at Mr Keenly.

'Er, Mr Keenly, I can't write that in the gap, sir.'

'Why not?' said Mr Keenly.

'Because I don't know for certain that the hat Billy is wearing is his hat. It doesn't say that it's his hat. So I can't write down, "His hat was blue" when I don't know if it was his hat.'

Mr Keenly frowned even more frownily, which meant that the small piece of skin between his two eyebrows made a kind of fold which Malcolm stared at and wondered, if he planted a sunflower seed in it, would it grow into a sunflower?

'Let's just say that it IS Billy's hat,' said Mr Keenly, and when he said 'IS' he did all the eye-opening, mouth-pushing, wiggly-finger things again.

Malcolm felt sweaty and uncomfortable.
And sad.

Crackersnacker looked at Malcolm and tried to help by beaming helpful feelings at him through his fingertips:

It didn't work.

'No, sir. I can't do that,' said Malcolm. 'That would be wrong. That's how you get questions wrong, sir. I don't want to get any of my questions wrong. My Uncle Gobb says that I must get all my questions right or I will end up as a good-for-nothing, standing about on street corners, expecting a free ride.'

'Well, Malcolm,' said Mr Keenly in his most-kindly-as-possible voice, 'I can tell you that the answer to the question is "blue". Billy's hat was blue. I've got the answers here and if you put "blue" in the gap, you'll get ... let me see ... one mark. Yes. One mark. How about that? One mark. Not bad, eh? Better than a kick up the bum.'

Malcolm could feel his eyes getting fizzy.

That's what happened when people said stuff to him that didn't fit with what he could see. Things got fizzy.

And sad.

'But, sir,' he said, 'the answer you've got on your piece of paper could be wrong.'

Crackersnacker said, 'Don't worry about it, Malc. It probably isn't wrong, you know. Just put "blue".'

And he tried to beam some more helpful feelings at Malc through his fingertips.

Just then two children on another table started practising licking each other's noses. They were called Ulla and Spaghetti.

Mr Keenly saw them with the eyes he had in the back of his head and said, 'Ulla, Spaghetti, could you do that nose-licking thing later, please. We're doing the Billy Worksheet thing now.'

He turned back to Malcolm.

'The answers I have on my piece of paper may be right, they may be wrong, Malcolm me old matey, but they are always THE answers. It doesn't matter if they are right or wrong, they are just the answers that you have to put. Billy's hat was blue. That's THE answer.'

(I think you can guess what he did with his eyes, mouth and finger when he said the word 'THE'.)

Then Mr Keenly walked on to help the next child.

Malcolm looked again at the worksheet.

Suddenly, to his amazement, he saw something else. At the very bottom in tiny, tiny writing, it said GOBB EDUCATION™

Gobb? Could it just possibly be something to do with ... Uncle Gobb?

'Hey Crackersnacker,' Malcolm whispered, 'look at that.'

Crackersnacker looked and saw the 'Gobb Education' writing too.

Crackersnacker put his finger on to his face so as to look like a serious person on TV and said, 'Could this be something to do with the person who wants you to do more homework and who you would like out of your house? The one who bamboozles and confuzles you, mm?'

Malcolm nodded.

Just then two children on another table started doing an experiment on how hard they could bite each other's fingers before the other one said, 'STOPPPPP!'

Malcolm looked at the next bit of writing on the worksheet.

It said: 'It was raining.'

And underneath that, it said:

'Why was Billy wearing a hat?'

Then there was a gap.

Malcolm started to think of all the reasons why Billy could be wearing a hat.

He turned to Crackersnacker.

'I've got several answers to why Billy is wearing a hat.'

He showed Crackersnacker his list.

He liked hats. His mum told him to

He liked __that__ hat.

He thought that when he walked about in that hat he looked COOL.

He hated wearing the hat but he thought that if he wore a hat people wouldn't notice the fact that he had cut his hair HIMSELF that day and it was all WONKY

70

'He liked wearing the hat because once a bully-kid had stolen it from him, and now wearing it showed the bully-kid that he wasn't afraid of him any more, yeah…'

Crackersnacker looked at Malcolm in a wondering sort of a way. 'Or you could just write, "He was wearing the hat because it was raining".'

Malcolm looked back at Crackersnacker.

Crackersnacker breathed in, nodded, looked again at Malcolm in an admiring sort of a way, and said, 'But, yeah, I get you, Malc, saying that it was because it was raining might be boring.'

Malcolm thought he had better choose

one of his answers pretty quick. Uncle Gobb
once told him that the thing about exams is that
it's all a matter of 'getting on well'. So here he
was – OK, it wasn't an exam – but he had to
'get on well'. Not like Ulla and Spaghetti licking
noses. They weren't 'getting on well'. Not like
Singalong and Freddy biting each other's fingers.
They weren't 'getting on well'.

In fact, up on the wall was the

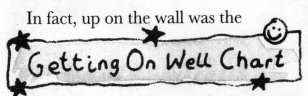

Every day Mr Keenly had to decide who was Getting On Well. AND who was Not Getting On Well.

Malcolm felt worried. He was near the bottom of the Getting On Well chart. He wasn't Getting On Well at all.

And this surprised him and made him sad.

He felt like he was Getting On Well all the time. Like right now, as he figured out all these interesting reasons about why Billy was wearing that hat, the hat which may or may not have been his.

74

So he Got On Well with it. He wrote down, 'Billy is wearing the hat because blue is the colour of his favourite football team.'

At the end of the lesson, everyone, even Ulla, Spaghetti, Singalong and Freddy, handed in their worksheets.

Malcolm looked up at the Worksheet Chart. This was another chart and it was next to the Getting On Well Chart . After the worksheets were marked by Janet, everyone's name was put at the right place on the

Worksheet Chart. If you got a good Worksheet mark, you were out in front. If you got a bad Worksheet mark, you were behind. 'Who is Janet?' you say. Janet helps. She is not called a helper though. She is called an 'Assistant'. And a very nice Assistant she is too. Janet likes Mr Keenly. Oh yes.

Uncle Gobb often said to Malcolm that he mustn't Be Behind.

Malcolm thought about that as he looked at the Worksheet chart.

In fact, thinking about Uncle Gobb telling him that he mustn't Be Behind made him upset. And angry. He was upset-angry. He was upsengry. And angrupset.

I must do something about Uncle Gobb, he thought...

He imagined that Uncle Gobb was standing in front of him.

Look here, Uncle Gobb, he said in his mind, if I wasn't behind, someone else would be behind. That's the whole point about 'in front' and 'behind'. As long as there's an 'in front' there has to be a 'behind'. Like me. Here's my front and here's my behind. 'We can't all be "in front", can we?'

(He said that last bit out loud, and Crackersnacker heard him.)

'No, Malc, we can't,' said Crackersnacker in his most helpful-hopeful voice.

Still, that answer about blue being the colour of Billy's favourite football team was a

surely. Maybe he might be 'in front' this time.

'Playtime,' called out Mr Keenly. 'Janet

will be with you for playtime today,' he said, 'and I'm asking her to make sure you're all very sensible – that includes you, Ulla, Spaghetti, Singalong and Freddy, and when she comes back with you, the head teacher has asked her to put all your names in the right place on the Behaving Sensibly at Playtime Chart.'

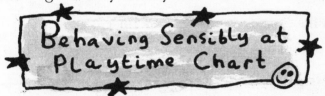

Janet nodded in a very serious way.

It was quite a big nod. Bigger than a quick nod. It was an I'm-taking-this-very-seriously-and-I-hope-you-are-too nod.

Malcolm sat trying to do a big nod too.

He thought, I'm taking this very seriously
and I hope you are too, as he sat there nodding.

'I saw that, Malcolm,' said Mr Keenly.

'Janet, make sure that Malcolm starts playtime very, very behind on the Behaving Sensibly at Playtime Chart. Off you go.'

'Oh no,' said Crackersnacker to Mr Keenly, 'Malcolm wasn't not Behaving Sensibly at Playtime. He was just practising his nodding. I know he was. He's like that. Really.'

'All right,' said Mr Keenly, 'I take your point.'

Why's he taking away my point? thought Malcolm. I thought I just got a point for writing 'blue' in the question about the hat.

All the children filed out and just as Malcolm walked past Mr Keenly and Janet, he discovered two incredible, amazing and stunning things.

CHAPTER 13
PART 1

The First Strange Thing

The first strange thing was that as he walked past Mr Keenly and Janet he heard Mr Keenly say to Janet, 'I can't stand these horrible charts. If I had my way, I'd pile them up in the playground and burn the diddly lot.'

MYSTERIOUSLY SHOCKING!!!

CHAPTER 13

PART 2

The Second Strange Thing

The second strange thing that Malcolm discovered as he walked past the charts was some very small writing at the bottom of one of them. You can guess what it said, can't you? I mean, if this was a piece of writing on a Worksheet and it said, 'What was written on the bottom of the chart?' and then there was a gap, you would be able to write something in the gap, wouldn't you?

Do you think the writing on the charts would say,

Roses are RED,
Violets are BLUE!
Most poems RHYME,
        This one doesn't ?

Do you think it would say,

THE moon is not a ~~dead~~ dead fish ?

Or do you think it would say,

GOBB EDUCATION™ ?

I'm going to leave you with that little problem until tomorrow.

I can't be sure it will be tomorrow, because I don't know how you're reading this book. You might be reading it yesterday.

Or on a bus.

Or on a bus yesterday.

Only YOU know.

And that is something you should treasure like you treasure the love of a good person.

PS – Malcolm did point it out to Crackersnacker though, so Crackersnacker is probably one other person who knows. I hope you don't mind about that. Crackersnacker seems like a mostly OK sort of a guy, don't you think?

CHAPTER 14

That Night

Malcolm, Tess and Uncle Gobb were having baked beans on toast.

'Tess,' said Uncle Gobb, 'the boy is having toast on beans. The beans are on the bottom. The toast is on top of the beans. You said quite clearly, we are having beans on toast and the boy is disobeying you. He is not doing as he's told. He is behaving in a rude, insolent and disrespectful way towards you. What are you going to do about it?'

Mum looked at Malcolm's plate.

'Oh come off it, Derek,' she said, 'it's still beans AND toast, isn't it? It's no big deal which way up it is, is it?'

'And that's it,' said Uncle Gobb, 'that's where we're going wrong. Years ago, if a parent said, "We're having beans on toast", we just got on with it, and we had our beans ON our toast. You know something, Tess? You know why we're falling behind? Because young people today think they can run before they can walk. I'm not against people having beans UNDER their toast but only after they've learned how to do beans ON toast first. First things first, Tess. Remember, the **DREAD SHED** is always with me. And when I say **"DREAD SHED"**, Malcolm, I mean a whole lot of **DREAD** for you.'

And he pointed fiercely at Malcolm's nose.

Malcolm munched his beans. And his toast. He thought, I don't want Uncle Gobb to bamboozle and confuzle me. If this goes on any longer I will have to think of a way to bamboozle and confuzle him. Then he'll leave, go, whoosh! I wonder if I will be able to bring about Uncle Gobb's downfall and humiliate him without destroying him? he thought. I'm just eating beans. And toast. It's no big deal which way I eat them, is it? But before he could say that to Uncle Gobb, his mum had something to say.

'Oh, come off it, Derek,' said Tess, 'the main reason why we're falling behind is because the fat cats have made off with the cream and there are no dairies left making milk.'

Uncle Gobb shook his head.

'Tess, my dear,' he said, 'I'VE BEEN TO CHINA.'

Tess said nothing.

Aha, thought Malcolm, that must have been a KILLER ANSWER: The 'I'VE BEEN TO CHINA' KILLER ANSWER. He tucked it away in the back of his mind, thinking that it could come in handy. Maybe he'd be out on the play-space at the end of the park and some big kid would come up to him and say, 'Don't try to be funny with me, Ponkyboy,' and he could cut back in quick with, 'MY DEAR, I'VE BEEN TO CHINA.'

Or maybe he'd be in the yellow bike shop staring at the bike that he would love to have if only Mum had the cash to buy it, and the man in the shop with the bony knees called Zegg (the knees aren't called Zegg, the man is called

Zegg) would say, 'If you're not buying that bike, move along and make room for someone who is, Ponkyboy.'

And Malcolm could say, '**MY DEAR, I'VE BEEN TO CHINA.**'

But why oh why oh why, you're wondering now, would the big kid in the park (probably Sandra the Big Kid. Or possibly Zilch the Big Kid) or Zegg call Malcolm 'Ponkyboy'?

Even Crackersnacker sometimes calls him Ponky or Ponkyboy, you know.

CHAPTER 15

Ponkyboy

Once when Malcolm was on television, the stunning, superb, beautiful most celebrityist celebrity to have ever appeared on television said to Malcolm, 'What is the name of the capital city of Italy?' and Malcolm paused, thought and then said, '**Ponky**.'

From that time on, everyone called him Ponkyboy.

I'm going to guess now that you have two more questions:

    1. Why was Malcolm on television?

    2. Why did he say '**Ponky**'?

I'm going to answer those questions:

    1. No one has ever found out why Malcolm was on television. One minute he wasn't on television. Then the next moment he was. It was possibly something to do with the fact that the director of 'A Question of Questions' turned to the Helper on the programme and said, 'Hey, Helper, we've got to find a kid for the next programme. Just get out

there and find me a kid.' And it so happens that the Helper was Tess's cousin (who was called Trinidad) and who was, believe it or not, that very evening seeing Tess and Malcolm.

It may have something to do with that.

Or not.

Remember, in life there are connections.

That was quite a **non-fiction**, important thing to say so I'll say it again.

Remember, in life there are connections.

2. Why did he say 'Ponky'?

No one has ever found out why Malcolm said 'Ponky'. One moment he wasn't saying Ponky. Then the next moment he was. It was possibly something to do with the fact that at the very moment the celebrityist celebrity (who was called Russell) asked Malcolm,

'What's the name of the capital of Italy?'

Malcolm was thinking of that rhyme,

'Inky Pinky Ponky,

The farmer bought a donkey,

The donkey died,

The farmer cried,

Inky Pinky Ponky.'

Now, of course this meant that he might have said any of the words from the rhyme:

'inky' or

‎ ‎ ‎ ‎ ‎ 'pinky' or

‎ ‎ ‎ ‎ ‎ ‎ ‎ ‎ ‎ 'the' or

‎ ‎ ‎ ‎ ‎ ‎ 'farmer' or

‎ ‎ ‎ 'bought' or

'a' or

'donkey' ...

... I don't need to go on, do I?

But, and this is important, the whole point is that Malcolm had only got to the end of the first line of 'Inky Pinky Ponky'. He was thinking 'Inky Pinky Ponky' and hadn't got to thinking, 'the farmer...' So he said the first thing that came into his mind, which was:

'Ponky!!!'

And the whole country, the whole world saw it.

And how they laughed. How they loved the boy who said that the capital of Italy was **Ponky**.

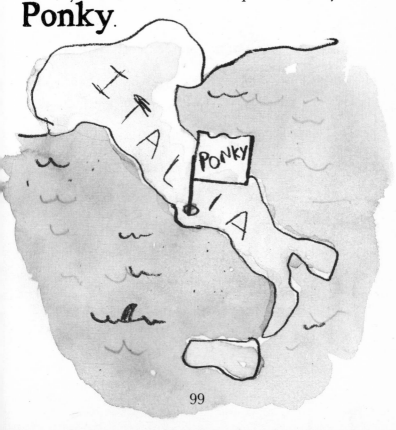

Well, they didn't love *him*. They loved the fact that it wasn't them who said Ponky. It made everyone feel that they were cleverer than the boy who said Ponky. In fact, they weren't loving him. They were loving themselves. They all felt much better now than they felt in the moment just before he said 'Ponky'.

And Russell looked at the audience in the studio and he looked at the audience at home (well, not really, he just looked at the camera) and said, 'Ponky, eh? Ponky, eh? Never mind, Ponky ... you got that one a bit wonky.'

And this became one of the most famous things that anyone ever said about anything. Yes, it's very famous when it says in Shakespeare, 'To be or not to be...' And it was very famous when Winston Churchill said that stuff about 'never in the field of human conflict...' though perhaps you don't remember that one. Or perhaps you do. How should I know?

But much more famous, much, much, much more famous was when Russell (who had the loveliest teeth in the world) said, 'Ponky, eh? Ponky, eh? Never mind, Ponky ... you got that one a bit wonky.'

There are very thick, heavy books called things like 'Dictionary of Quotations' or 'Dictionary of famous things that people said which changed the world forever' and if you look in books like that, you'll see it says,

'Russell: "Ponky, eh? Ponky, eh? Never mind, Ponky ... you got that one a bit wonky."'

However, I should say that in the **DICTIONARY OF KILLER ANSWERS** it says:

No one knows why the **DICTIONARY OF KILLER ANSWERS** has got it wrong, but if you find a copy, could you please do me a favour and write to them telling them what it should be? They don't take any notice when I write to them because they say that I don't cut my toenails often enough.

CHAPTER 16

After The Beans

Malcolm finished his toast and beans. His mind wandered back to the classroom and the mystery of why it said Gobb Education on the bottom of the Worksheet and on the bottom of the Charts.

'Uncle Gobb?'
said Malcolm.

ROME!

shouted Uncle Gobb.

I should tell you that Uncle Gobb was very ashamed of Malcolm. When he came home from the TV programme that day, Uncle Gobb was sitting with his head in his hands, sobbing.

'Oh for goodness' sake, everyone in the whole world knows that the capital of Italy is Rome, but our little nincompoop says it's "Ponky". That's the problem. Young people today don't know anything. They know nothing at all. All those facts, all that knowledge – and they know none of it. I'VE BEEN TO CHINA.'

When Malcolm saw and heard the way Uncle Gobb was that day, that was the beginning of why he started to plot how to bamboozle and confuzle him.

Meanwhile, to try and get some facts and knowledge into Malcolm, Uncle Gobb worked out an interesting scheme.

We will find out what this interesting scheme is in just a moment.

We will be back with the baked beans and toast.

CHAPTER 17

Uncle Gobb's Interesting Scheme

Malcolm finished his toast on beans.

(I know he's already finished his beans once. What I mean is that we're still with him exactly as he finishes his beans.)

Then, as part of Uncle Gobb's interesting scheme, he barked questions at Malcolm:

'WHAT'S FOUR PLUS FOUR?'

4 + 4 = ?

'WHERE'S EGYPT?'

'WHERE DOES THE

'WHO WAS THE PRESIDENT OF THE UNITED STATES OF AMERICA?'

'ARE WE?'

'WHEN'S TEA-TIME?'

'WHO IS?'

'CAN IT?'

EQUATOR END?'

It was Malcolm's job to fire back the answers.

The trouble was that some of the questions didn't make sense, and so Uncle Gobb got sadder and sadder and angrier and angrier and redder and redder until in the end everyone was very upset.

When Uncle Gobb asked, 'Who was the President of the United States?'

Malcolm said,

And Uncle Gobb shouted at him,

'I'M ASKING THE QUESTIONS ROUND HERE!!!'

Which didn't help.

So, Mum said, 'Derek, be a dear. Just think up some other way of doing questions, eh?'

'All right then,' said Uncle Gobb, 'here is my new way of doing questions: if there is anything, Malcolm, you don't know the answer to, ask me.'

Malcolm thought for a bit and then said, 'Is there anything lighter than light?'

Uncle Gobb said, 'That's a very good question, boy. That's an excellent question. I like that question. It's a question that is very interesting and mind-consuming. It's one of the best questions I've ever heard in all my life. And **I'VE BEEN TO CHINA**.'

Aha, thought Malcolm. There are times

when Uncle Gobb isn't the most annoying, boring person in the world. He is the most stuck person in the world.

'All right then,' said Uncle Gobb, 'the best way to do questions is for me to think of a question. I then get you to ask me that very same question and then I will answer it. So, my boy, supposing you wanted to know … er … um … what fuel is burned in an internal combustion engine, you say to me, "What fuel is burned in the internal combustion engine?" Off you go then.'

Malcolm left the room.

Uncle Gobb shouted after him.

'No, no, no! Come back. I didn't mean,

"off you go". I meant, ask the question.'

Malcolm said, 'OK.'

This is how it went after that:

Uncle Gobb: 'Who won the Men's 100 metres at the 2012 Olympics? would be an interesting question, Malcolm.

Malcolm: Uncle Gobb, who won the Men's 100 metres at the 1912 Olympics?

Uncle Gobb: 2012.

Malcolm, Oh, that's interesting, 2012 won the Men's 100 metres at the 1912 Olympics, eh?

Uncle Gobb: The question I suggested you ask was: 'Who won the Men's 100 metres at the 2012 Olympics?'

Malcolm: Oh, right, but while we're on

1912, who did win the Men's 100 metres at the 1912 Olympics?

Uncle Gobb (shouting): I HAVE NO IDEA!!! I don't even know if there was an Olympics in 1912. We're not talking about 1912.

Malcolm: No, I know you're not, but I am. But if you don't know the answer to the question, then I'm not really learning anything, Uncle Gobb.

You might be wondering at this moment if Malcolm was saying these things to annoy Uncle Gobb. I certainly am.

Uncle Gobb: But if you asked me the question about the 2012 Olympics you would learn something for a change.

Malcolm: But I know who won the Men's 100 metres in the 2012 Olympic Games. It was Usain Bolt.

Uncle Gobb (shouting): YOU REALLY DON'T GET IT, DO YOU? I'm trying to teach you something here. I'm trying to teach you how to ask questions. I'm trying to teach you some really interesting answers and you muck the whole thing up. We're falling behind, boy, and I'VE BEEN TO CHINA!!!

This explains why, back in Chapter 16, Uncle Gobb shouted 'Rome!'

He was imagining that he had asked

Malcolm to ask him that one key question that Russell with the nice teeth asked.

And there was the right answer: 'Rome!'

But in fact, Malcolm was going to ask him, 'Why did it say Gobb Education on the bottom of the Getting On Well Chart and the Worksheet Chart and the Behaving Sensibly at Playtime Chart?'

But just then, Mum came in and said, 'Bed.'

Malcolm felt that he needed to share all this with Crackersnacker, but Crackersnacker wasn't there at that precise moment.

Which is a pity, Malcolm thought.

So he was sad.

CHAPTER 18

Bed

In bed, Malcolm brought into his mind all the times he had seen 'Gobb Education' while he had been at school.

The more he looked at them in his mind, the more the word 'Gobb' seemed to blur and mix with Uncle Gobb's face.

The next moment Malcolm was in Binner Market with Crackersnacker.

Binner was where Tess and Malcolm and Crackersnacker lived.

You might be wondering why I didn't say,

Tess and Malcolm and Crackersnacker AND Uncle Gobb.

That's because on Uncle Gobb's little white address card that he handed out to people it said,

Uncle Gobb c/o
The Cow Club
London

So Uncle Gobb didn't really think he belonged in Binner. He thought he belonged to The Cow Club.

Back at Binner Market, Malcolm
found that he and Crackersnacker were
walking down the road looking at the stalls.
There was the man who sold jeans
but today … how odd! … he seemed to be
selling a kind of dolls' house model.
'C'mon,' he shouted, 'let's see the
colour of your money. Look at this one,
tasty or what?'

Over there on another stall was the man who usually sold 'Fresh Veg.', and today, like the jeans man, he was selling some kind of dolls' house thing. Just one, sitting right in the middle of his stall, just where you'd expect to see his potatoes and carrots.

'Lovely jubbly. Lovely jubbly,' he shouted.

And so it was across stall after stall, all of them selling just one dolls' house thing.

And then, in the middle of it all, was Uncle Gobb.

He was sitting in a chair that was on a platform which was being carried down the middle of the road by four very strong men. He nodded and smiled to everyone, and people looked up and nodded back at him. Every now and then he threw some money in the direction of the stall holders but he didn't seem interested in buying anything.

Malcolm and Crackersnacker followed after him and it was then that Malcolm realised that he was in a dream. The question is, though, he thought, am I in MY dream, or am I in someone else's dream? If it's someone else's dream, whose dream? And if it's someone else's, how will I ever find out whose dream it is?

While he was thinking this, he realised that he and Crackersnacker were getting closer and closer to the stall at the end of Binner Market and to his surprise, now it was Uncle Gobb selling a dolls' house too but ... but ... but ... it wasn't a dolls' house at all. It was his school. Janet and Mr Keenly were crying and shouting, 'No, no, no…'

But Uncle Gobb was now laughing and nodding more and more and pointing in all directions at the same time...

Crackersnacker whispered to Malcolm, 'Quick, you've got to get rid of him. Do it now! Do some bamboozling and confuzling!'

Then it all went blank.

CHAPTER 19

Back at School: Malcolm Talking With
Crackersnacker In The Playground After
School – And A Surprise
(It's OK, It's A Good One).

'Listen, Crackersnacker, it's all beginning to make sense. I've a funny feeling,' said Malcolm, 'all this stuff going on is something to do with Uncle Gobb.'

'Yes,' said Crackersnacker, 'and not Billy with the Blue Hat.'

'Exactly,' said Malcolm, rubbing the side of his nose.

What Malcolm didn't realise was that at that moment, his nose had turned into Aladdin's Lamp and as he rubbed his nose, it summoned up a Genie.

The Genie appeared in a puff of smoke …

... and stood in front of Malcolm and Crackersnacker and said, 'I am the Genie of the Magic Lamp. I got tired of being in that Aladdin story year after year after year so I thought things might be a bit more lively if I moved out. You can't imagine how sick I am of being in those plays and pantomimes where I jump up and everyone claps. Yawn yawn. So here I am: The Genie of Malcolm's Magic Nose. I am at your service. Your wish is my command.'

Crackersnacker laughed. 'This is amazing, Ponkyboy. Like really amazing. Like really, really amazing.'

Malcolm looked at the Genie and said, 'Wow! You came out of my nose!'

The Genie raised his hand. 'No, there's no need to get all hero-worshippy and silly about it. I'm just an ordinary genie doing my job. What can I do for you?'

'Me?' said Crackersnacker.

The Genie looked at him. 'I don't want to sound nasty, young man, but just cast your mind back a moment and ask yourself whose nose was being rubbed in the moment before I appeared in a puff of smoke?'

'Ponkyboy's?' said Crackersnacker.

'Yes,' said the Genie, 'so look, I can hold you on the line if you have another request, but in the meantime, I'm going back to the original caller.'

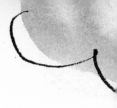

Malcolm was playing with the Genie's smoke, running his hands through it as if it was some kind of water.

The Genie moved closer.

Malcolm looked up. 'Oh yes, my wish is your command. What do I wish for? Ho hum humble hum ... hmmmm.'

Crackersnacker may well have been peaky, but he was also pretty sharp. Not as sharp as a very sharp knife but still pretty sharp. He said, 'What you were saying about Uncle Gobb, an' that.'

'What was I saying?' said Malcolm.

'The stuff about how you thought it was all to do with him.'

'Yes...'

'Well,' said Crackersnacker, 'we could get your Genie – him – to find out more stuff.'

'This "stuff-stuff" is getting confusing,' said the Genie. 'I need more details than that.'

Malcolm slowly explained what he had noticed about the Worksheets and the Charts.

'What I need to know is whether the Gobb Education person is the same as Uncle Gobb. Or not,' he said.

'Aha,' said the Genie. 'Oh, I should say,' he interrupted himself, 'that I have to say "aha" like that because it's a kind of genie groove that I have to gig to. Genies always do "aha". But never mind that,' he went on, 'remember, if you have the knowledge, it may lead you to do **TERRIBLE AND DANGEROUS THINGS**.'

'Sounds brill,' said Crackersnacker. 'I love terrible and dangerous.'

'Er … me too …' said Malcolm uncertainly but he didn't want Crackersnacker to think he was uncertain, so he said it again, really fiercely. As fierce as a Norse God like Thor or a Greek demon like Medusa: 'Me tooooooo! Oh yes.'

(And he opened his eyes wide, pushed out his mouth and did a wiggly line thing with his finger.)

'Well,' said the Genie, 'I will investigate this whole Gobb story, put a girdle round the earth in forty minutes or forty seconds – I forget which – and come back to you in a thrice.'

'Thrice?' said Crackersnacker. 'What sort of car is a Thrice?'

'I know not of what you speak,' said the Genie.

Then he leaned forward and said in a hushed voice, 'Every now and then, boys, I like talking in my old book voice. You may have no idea what I'm talking about when I do that, but wow it's fun. OK, so I've got my instructions. I'll get on with it. Gobb, name, details, er ... going forward.'

And the Genie disappeared.

Malcolm turned to Crackersnacker. 'What did he mean "going forward"?'

Crackersnacker looked wise. Peaky but wise with it.

'"Going forward" is what all important people say nowadays, Malc. Everyone's going forward.'

'What if they want to go back?' said Malcolm.

'Well, they go back, going forward, don't they?' said Crackersnacker.

'Brill,' said Malcolm.

They sat saying nothing for a while thinking about *going forward,*

going back,

going sideways,

going up,

going down,

going round and round,

going crazy ...

and just going.

'I'm just wondering,' said Crackersnacker, 'do we have any idea how long the Genie is going to take before he comes back with the information that is going to help us be terrible and dangerous?'

'Nope,' said Malcolm, 'this whole genie wotsit is new to me … but I'm wondering if he's going to help us get rid of Uncle Gobb.'

'That's where your bamboozling stuff comes in,' said Crackersnacker.

'Is it?' said Malcolm.

So the two went on sitting there …

… and you can make this next bit last as long or as short as you like because that's the end of the chapter.

CHAPTER 20

The Wait – For As Long As You Like

CHAPTER 21

The Genie Comes Back After The Wait

There was a puff of smoke …

… and the Genie appeared before Malcolm and Crackersnacker.

'My wish is your command,' he called out to them.

'I think you've done that bit,' said

Malcolm. 'I've done the wish, it turned into a command, you went off, and now you're back to tell us what's going on.'

'That's a very good point, Malc,' said Crackersnacker.

The Genie glanced at a piece of paper he was carrying.

'I'm so sorry, I must have turned back the pages of the script. I'll do that arrival again.'

'No, no need to bother,' said Crackersnacker.

'Right,' said the Genie, 'then what I found out is that Uncle Gobb is the evil mastermind behind everything. He's like a farmer in charge of sheep. Or a greengrocer in charge of tomatoes, or the man in Mike's Fish Bar in charge of chips.'

'Everything?' said Malcolm. 'What, even that time I got told off for spitting out chewing gum on the bus on the school trip?'

'Yes,' said the Genie.

'Even that time when Mum bought some apples from Binner Market and one of them was a bit brown inside?'

'Yes,' said the Genie.

Just then Uncle Gobb turned up.

'You're not the only ones who can summon up Genies,' he shouted at the boys. 'Watch this!'

Uncle Gobb started rubbing his face. Yes, his shiny forehead, cheeks and chin. As he did it, he muttered, 'Italy, Spittaly, Spain was Hungary;

Spain ate Turkey dipped in Greece.'

Aha, thought Malcolm, that's the secret of the polishing. This is all starting to make sense…

Then,

PHUFFFF!!!

'I am the immensely powerful, all-seeing wrinkly old genie with glasses. Heh heh heh heh! Whatever you do, I know what you're doing and even if I don't know, I have ways of finding out. I am the amazing Doctor Roop the Doop, doop dee doop. My command is my command.'

Some of this made sense to Malcolm and Crackersnacker and some of it didn't. For a start, how come when Malcolm had watched Uncle Gobb rub his face in the bathroom, a genie had NOT appeared?

Then he figured it out:

It was because in the bathroom Uncle Gobb had NOT said, 'Italy Spittaly, Spain was Hungary; Spain ate Turkey dipped in Greece'.

Uncle Gobb was looking pretty pleased with himself. 'Hiya, Uncle Gobb,' he said to himself, 'you're looking good.'

'I,' said Malcolm's Genie, 'have all the information on this person. I know what he is up to, I know what he is doing going forward.'

'Pssst,' said Malcolm, 'there's that going forward thing again.'

'I know,' said Crackersnacker, 'I noticed that too.'

But Doctor Roop the Doop, doop dee doop, wasn't going to hang about listening to this nonsense, and instead, he jumped at Malcolm's genie. In his hands were two metal plugs, like the ones you stick into a computer, and before anyone could stop him, he stuck these into Malcolm's Genie's head.

'And now,' cackled the Doctor Roop, 'I will get to know what you're thinking, as these plugs are connected up to my international network of networks. In a split second I will receive a text informing me of your innermost thoughts and plans.'

Everyone waited for the text.

They waited a long time.

In the time they waited, everyone imagined what the Genie of Malcolm's Nose might be thinking. Here are some of the things they thought:

They deserve a special chapter.

CHAPTER 22

What They Imagined That The Genie Of
Malcolm's Nose Might Be Thinking

① He's thinking about The
Thousand and One Nights,
that marvellous, amazing set of
Stories including ALi BABA
and Aladdin.

② He's thinking about 'CRUMBLE'
a particularly delicious chocolate bar
which is FULL of crumbly chocolate.

③ He is Thinking about
thinking.

④ He is thinking about US.

⑤ ~~Stuart~~

⑥ He's thinking that
FRENCH ▯ PEOPLE don't
call water melon' a kind of melon.

⑦ Thank YOU for
giving us a special new chapter.

CHAPTER 23

Strange

'Hmm, very strange,' said the Doctor, 'no text.'

'I can explain,' said Malcolm's Genie, 'I have no inner thoughts. All my thoughts are outer thoughts. You have been defeated, again, you cruel but useless little man.'

'Again?' said Malcolm. 'Have you done this sort of thing before? Do you two know each other?'

'Oh yes,' said Malcolm's Genie, 'I can tell you that this is none other than Doctor Roop the Doop, doop dee doop, the Evil Power summoned by Uncle Gobb to run the minds of 38 per cent of the world's population. But he is always hungry for more, more, more. He won't stop until he gets control of all the minds, but I, the Genie of the Magic Lamp –'

'Magic Nose,' interrupted Malcolm.

'– the Magic Nose, you're right: I, the Genie of the Magic Nose, along with you two brave boys, possess the one power that will stop the evil Doctor once and for all.'

'What power is that?' whispered Crackersnacker, who was getting quite hungry now, and wanted to go back to the cloakroom to pick up his Crumbles Bar – one of those bars which are made of chocolate but there's some

special crumbly
chocolate inside
... oh, you knew
that already.

CRUMBLES BAR

'I'm not
really sure about
the one power that will stop the evil Doctor once
and for all, just now. Not at the moment,' said
the Genie, 'but it sounded really good when I
said it, don't you think?'

'Yes, it did sound good, but did you find
out about the name of Gobb being on the end
of the Worksheets and everything?' Malcolm
asked urgently.

'I did,' said the Genie.

'And?' said Crackersnacker.

'At this moment in time,' said the Genie, 'I can't quite figure if the name "Gobb" is on the Worksheets because they are Uncle Gobb's Worksheets or if Doctor Roop the Doop, doop dee doop, put the Gobb name there. But between them, believe me, they did it.'

Now, you might be wondering what Doctor Roop the Doop, doop dee doop, was doing while all this chat was going on.

I'll tell you.

He was fulminating.

FULMINATING –
AN EXPLANATION

'Fulminating' means he was muttering and grunting and planning and scheming and breathing and spitting. Spitting is not an absolute must as part of fulminating and is reallly rather unpleasant. I'm sorry I mentioned it, but becauses it really was something that Doctor Roop the Doop, doop dee doop did, I thought I had to.

Another thing you might be wondering is, what was Uncle Gobb doing all this time?

And that is an even more interesting question.

Uncle Gobb was preparing to destroy Malcolm and Crackersnacker.

Deep inside his brain, something had made him realise that it was Malcolm (and now his friend too, who had been so stupid as to join with Malcolm in this whole stupid, stupid, stupid business), who stood in his way.

Here he was trying to improve the world, and there was Malcolm asking all the wrong questions or no questions and answering the wrong answers or the right answers at the wrong time, sticking his nose into things to do with the name of Gobb and Doctor Roop the Doop, doop dee doop, and it was slowing everything down, stopping him getting on with making the world a place where people could be nice. Rich people would be nice to poor people and poor people would be nice to rich people. That's all he wanted.

It came to Uncle Gobb in a flash.

Malcolm and Crackersnacker must be put in the **DREAD SHED**, out of which no one had ever come. Yes, the **DREAD SHED** that was like Alcatraz, an island in the middle of the San Francisco Bay from which no one had ever escaped – apart from Clint Eastwood in a movie.

Uncle Gobb turned to Doctor Roop the Doop, doop dee doop, and whispered something.

I can tell you what he whispered but if you asked Malcolm and Crackersnacker, they wouldn't be able to tell you.

Uncle Gobb whispered, '**DREAD SHED**.'

(It's at this point in the story, you probably understand there are two plans going on:

1. Malcolm wanting to bamboozle and confuzle Uncle Gobb, so as to get rid of him.

2. Uncle Gobb thinking about how to do bad things to Malcolm. And if that meant bad things happening to Crackersnacker too, so be it.)

This means:

CONFLICT!!!!!

and the

DREAD SHEDDDD!!!!

CHAPTER 24

The Last Battle

From far off came the sound of the rumbling of castors.

The **DREAD SHED** was approaching the playground.

Uncle Gobb moved slowly and threateningly towards Malcolm. Doctor Roop the Doop, doop dee doop, moved slowly and threateningly towards Crackersnacker.

Malcolm's Genie, who, according to legend, should have been defending the two boys with one of those great curly swords called 'scimitars', had found a long mirror and was doing some kind of exercise routine in front of it so that he could observe his muscles getting bigger and smaller along his arms, along his legs, across his shoulders and down his front.

159

'I thought you said that my wish was your command,' said Malcolm.

'Yes,' said the Genie, 'but that was before I found this mirror. I am seriously impressed with the way I've bulked up,' he said. 'Just look at those biceps.'

'We're finished now,' said Crackersnacker, 'done for. We're dead meat.'

Uncle Gobb put his hand out to Doctor Roop de Doop, doop dee doop and held back his ever-onward rush.

'Before you disappear forever into the hell that is the **DREAD SHED**,' said Uncle Gobb, 'I want to explain one more thing to you, Malcolm.'

'Oh shwash and shwosh,' whispered Malcolm to Crackersnacker, 'his explanations are the worst of the lot. He goes on and on and on and on. I bet he says something about CHINA.'

'This school,' said Uncle Gobb with a great sneery leery look on his face, 'this school was built by the same people who abolished the DREAD SHEDS. And that, as my dear, dear father would say, was where the trouble started. It was schools like this, full of boys like you. You're what's gone wrong. You, you, you.'

'Uncle Gobb, you're doing that spitting thing again,' said Malcolm.

'How do you mean, "again"? Have I done

the spitting thing before?' said Uncle Gobb with
a worried edge to his voice.

'Oh, yes, Uncle Gobb,' said Malcolm
menacingly. 'I didn't want to mention it, but it is
an example of bad hygiene. We learned about it
in Science, didn't we, Crackersnacker?'

'Yep,' said Crackersnacker, as menacingly as possible in that one short word, 'yep'.

'I've tried everything I can to make this school better,' said Uncle Gobb. 'Do you know about my Gobb Education Force, who are ready whenever I ask them to rush in here and find out what's gone wrong? You've seen all the wonderful sheets and charts and posters that Doctor Roop and I have made…'

Crackersnacker nodded very noddingly at Malcolm when Uncle Gobb mentioned that.

So Malcolm had been right.

AHA!!!!

and

AHA!!!

again.

Uncle Gobb carried on: '... I even saved the very last **DREAD SHED** from destruction. This is all about making things better. You've even been in my dream, haven't you, boy? You were there the other day. You saw what I was trying to do. Yes. I've done all I can, all I can, all I can ...'

As he said this, Uncle Gobb started bringing the fist of his right hand slap, slap, slap right into the palm of his left hand.

SLAP!!!
SLAP!!!
SLAP!!!

Doctor Roop the Doop, doop dee doop, started growling and preparing more metal plugs to stick into the heads of Malcolm and Crackersnacker.

Crackersnacker turned to Malcolm, 'This is where you need to bring about the downfall of Uncle Gobb and –'

'Yeah, yeah, yeah, I know,' interrupted Malcolm, 'I'm just working on it.'

CHAPTER 25

Working On It

$$\frac{(45 - 23) \times y (2 - 2)}{(w^2 \, w^3 \, w^4) \, G}$$

etc...

Add **a b**it, take ~~away~~

away   A BIT...

$$\sqrt{9 \times 2 \times 100,000}$$

$\times 45\cancel{5}\cancel{3}$...

ETC...

ETC...

CHAPTER 26

A Sad Chapter

No matter how much working-on-it stuff went on, I'm afraid to say that this was the moment that we've all been dreading.

That word –

DREADING

– should give you a clue for what is about to happen …

Doctor Roop the Doop, doop dee doop, grabbed Crackersnacker and Uncle Gobb grabbed Malcolm, opened the door of the

DREAD SHED, pushed them inside and closed the door behind them.

168

CHAPTER 27

Part Of The Chorus Of An Old French Song

'Ohé ohé matelot,
matelot navigue sur les flots.'

The tune for this chorus is rather jolly even though the song is about some sailors who want to eat a little boy. The reason why it's turned up at this point in the story is because Malcolm and Crackersnacker know this song from their French lessons. Mr Keenly sings it very well. Janet likes the way Mr Keenly sings it. Malcolm and Crackersnacker sing the song whenever things aren't looking too good. Especially as it's about some sailors who want to eat a little boy. Like I said. They want to fry him before they eat him. I'm sorry about this. It's not my song. I didn't make it up. So it's not my fault.)

Things aren't looking too good for Malcolm and Crackersnacker at the moment.

Singing the song helps them think of something to make things better.

We'll see if things work out better for them in the next chapter.

I hope so.

CHAPTER 28

I'm Afraid Not – Not In This Chapter

CHAPTER 29

Don't Be Too Downhearted

'What happens in the **DREAD SHED**?' said Malcolm.

'You get the cane,' said Crackersnacker.

'What is that,' said Malcolm, 'some kind of present?'

'Nope,' said Crackersnacker, 'it's the whacks, the beats, a lickin'. They beat you with a stick.'

'Why?' said Malcolm.

'I don't know why,' said Crackersnacker, 'something to do with getting better.'

'Better than what?' said Malcolm.

'Better than you were before,' said Crackersnacker.

'Oh good,' said Malcolm, 'let's get the cane, then.'

'No, no, no,' said Crackersnacker, 'it really, really hurts.'

'And that makes you better?' said Malcolm.

'That's what they say,' said Crackersnacker.

Malcolm and Crackersnacker sat in the dark of the **DREAD SHED** for a while.

CHAPTER 30

Dark

This page is dark to show you how dark it was inside the **DREAD SHED**.

I can't see Malcolm or Crackersnacker, so you can see it was pretty dark.

CHAPTER 31

A Good Ending

Malcolm moved a bit closer to Crackersnacker. 'I don't like it in here. I want to get out.'

'But no one's ever escaped from here apart from Clint Eastwood in a movie.'

'I think that was Alcatraz,' said Malcolm, 'this is the **DREAD SHED**.'

'Ah yes,' said Crackersnacker, 'can you remember how Clint Eastwood got out of Alcatraz?'

'Yes,' said Malcolm, 'he spooned his way out.'

'Well that's it!' said Crackersnacker excitedly, 'we spoon our way out. What sort of spoon did he have?'

'I think it was a little spoon,' said Malcolm.

'Oh blow it,' said Crackersnacker, 'we haven't got a little spoon.'

A voice came from outside:

'ARE YOU TWO SORRY?'

It was Uncle Gobb.

The boys looked at each other.

'Are we sorry?' they whispered.

They shrugged.

Malcolm called back.

'We don't know.'

Uncle Gobb shouted back from outside.

'Well you're staying in there till you're sorry and until you know WHY you're sorry.'

'Phew!' said Malcolm. 'That's a hard one. I don't mind being sorry but I have no idea WHY I'm sorry.'

'Neither do I,' said Crackersnacker.

The boys sat in the dark some more.

Then Malcolm said, 'Crackersnacker, shut

your eyes really hard.'

He did.

'Now open them.'

He did.

'Can you see anything at all?'

'Yes,' said Crackersnacker, 'I can see a little line. Over there.'

'Me too,' said Malcolm, 'let's feel our way over there and see what's what.'

So the two boys crept across the floor of the Dread Shed towards the line.

'If you feel here,' said Crackersnacker, who was touching the line of light, 'it feels like the bottom of a door.'

Malcolm felt too … and then he pushed.

And the moment he pushed, the door opened.

That's because it WAS a door.

The door opened out into … more or less the same place as they were before Uncle Gobb and Doctor Roop pushed them in.

The boys looked at each other.

'It's not supposed to be that easy,' said Crackersnacker. 'We should have been in there for about twenty years, getting thinner and thinner and then in the end we either die, or Robin Hood rescues us, or we spoon our way out like Clint Eastwood did.'

'And to think: we just opened the door!' said Malcolm.

Just then Uncle Gobb came round the end of the Dread Shed with Doctor Roop and shouted, 'How did you two get out?'

'We opened the door,' said Malcolm.

'Impossible!' said Uncle Gobb. 'No one ever escapes from the Dread Shed. It's like Alcatraz.'

'We did,' said Crackersnacker.

'But how?' said Uncle Gobb, who was by now seriously flustered and blustered and mustard. 'None of my plans go wrong.'

'Yeah, but this one did,' said Crackersnacker, 'we did what people usually do with a door. We opened it…'

'…and then we walked out,' said Malcolm.

'I can't think how that happened,' said Uncle Gobb.

'It was because it was a door,' said Crackersnacker.

'So it opened,' said Malcolm.

'I expect it shuts as well,' said Crackersnacker.

'That's because it's a door,' said Malcolm.

'ENOUGH!!!!' shouted Uncle Gobb, 'Right, that was your last chance! Doctor Roop, we'll have to do it with our bare hands!'

BARE HANDS???!!!!!!

Malcolm looked to his Genie for help, but it was no good, he was doing press-ups. He was only on number forty-nine.

Crackersnacker fell to his knees.

'Then I crave a last boon.'

'What's that?' whispered Malcolm. 'What's with the cravey boony thing?'

'Oh I know,' said Doctor Roop the Doop, doop dee doop – who was a very old Genie – 'let me explain, it's what they do in old stories. When they're just about to die, they say, "I crave a last boon". It means, "I want a last wish".'

'So why don't they say, "I want a last wish"?' said Malcolm.

'Because it's in old stories,' said Doctor Roop.

'But this is a new story,' said Malcolm.

'Never mind that,' said Crackersnacker, 'I still want to crave a last boon.'

Uncle Gobb pondered on that one for a moment.

'I like old stories,' he said, 'and so, young knave, thou mayst crave one last boon.'

'What about my electric metal plugs?' said Doctor Roop, 'when do I get to use them?'

'Hold back, good doctor, your time will come,' said Uncle Gobb.

Crackersnacker winked at Malcolm and said, 'And, sire, may this last boon be a QUESTION? A question that we might ask of YOU?'

'Indeed forsooth,' said Uncle Gobb, who was beginning to enjoy himselfe talkinge in thisse olde waye.

Crackersnacker winked at Malcolm again, though Malcolm had no idea what all the winking was about.

'Don't you see,' said Crackersnacker clevernesslishly, 'this is it … this is it, Ponkyboy.'

As this is getting quite exciting and confusing at the same time, I think we need a very short rest.

Zz zzzZZZ

186

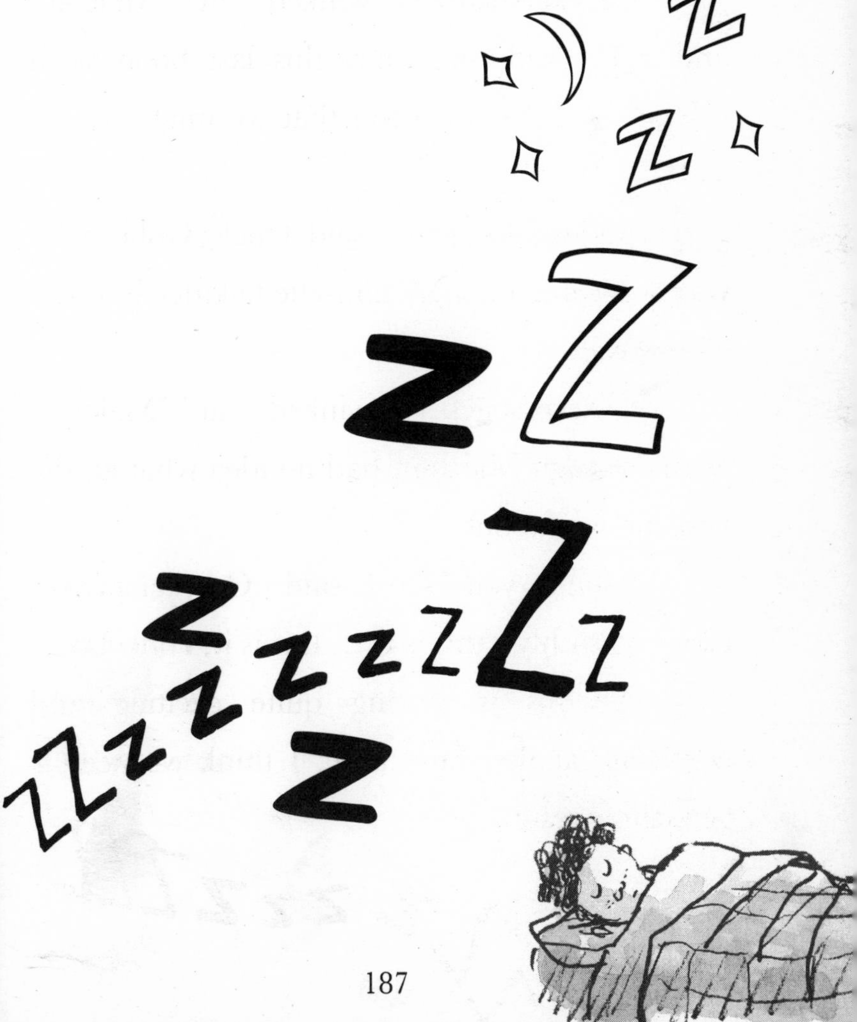

CHAPTER 32

Another Aha!!!

'Malc, don't you get it? Do the Billy Blue Hat thing!'

'What do you mean?' said Malcolm.

'Doctor Roop the Doop, doop dee doop, won't be able to do the Billy Blue Hat thing. NOR WILL UNCLE GOBB!!!' said Crackersnacker.

'Oh they diddly will,' said Malcolm.

'No, no, no,' said Crackersnacker, 'they won't know how to do all that roundabouty stuff that you say. And that will bamboozle and confuzle THEM. You know what I mean.'

'Do I?' said Malcolm, looking at Doctor Roop the Doop, who was holding some electric plugs and moving towards them.

'Yes,' shouted Crackersnacker desperately, 'not the Billy's-hat-is-blue thing, not the he's-wearing-a-hat-because-it's-raining. Your stuff. Your brilliant stuff, Ponkyboy. Go on, quick, before Gobb's genie sticks the plugs in us…'

There was a silence while Malcolm did some hard thinking …

… then he shouted:

'HOW DO YOU KNOW THAT THE HAT THAT BILLY IS WEARING IS HIS OWN HAT?!!!!'

Doctor Roop the Doop, doop dee doop, stopped.

Right there.

In his tracks.

He was absolutely still, going forward.

I mean he wasn't going forward, going forward.

'And, and, and…' Malcolm hesitated … he turned to Uncle Gobb, 'is Billy wearing the hat because once a bully-kid had stolen it from him, and now wearing it showed the bully-kid that he wasn't afraid of him anymore, yeah?'

There was more silence.

Uncle Gobb cleared his throat. His face went red.

He didn't know the answer.

He just stood still, spluttering.

And muttering.

And guttering.

And buttering.

In fact, he spluttered and muttered and guttered and buttered himself to a standstill.

A STANDSTILL!!!

He was utterly bamboozled and confuzled!

'See that,' whispered Crackersnacker, 'you know what that means, Malc?'

'What?' said Malcolm.

'It's his downfall. And I'm pretty sure he's going to leave us alone now,' said Crackersnacker, 'that's a major, major, major thingy you've done there, Ponkyboy!'

CHAPTER 33

The Standstill Means That's It. Or Is It?

Something very important happened straight after Uncle Gobb's standstill. Doctor Roop disappeared in a puff of smoke. Uncle Gobb had no more power over Doctor Roop. Just like a stone has no power over the frog sitting on it.

RIBBET.

With Doctor Roop gone, Malcolm's Genie didn't see much point in hanging about either. He disappeared off in a puff of smoke too.

Crackersnacker whispered to Malcolm, 'Maybe they go off to some sort of Genie Cafe and wait there till next time they get called.'

Just then, Malcolm's mum appeared. 'Oh, Derek, I didn't know you were picking up Malcolm...'

Uncle Gobb was still in his standstill. So he couldn't answer. Crackersnacker winked. Malcolm turned his face into a question mark.

'He can't move,' said Crackersnacker. 'All you have to do now is go home and you've got what you've wanted all along. You've got rid of

him, Ponkyboy!'

Malcolm looked at his mum. 'C'mon, Mum. I want to get home. Sofa Soccer's on TV.'

They started walking down the street away from Uncle Gobb.

'What's that?' said Mum.

'Celebrities sit on sofas trying to score goals with a mini-football,' Malcolm said.

'What do they use for goals?' Mum asked.

'The sofas,' said Malcolm.

They were getting further and further away from Uncle Gobb, who was still very still in his standstill. Crackersnacker winked and nodded at Malcolm and looked back over his shoulder. They both looked back at Uncle Gobb.

But that was a

BIG MISTAKE.

Mum noticed what Malcolm and Crackersnacker did. She turned round and called to Uncle Gobb, 'Pop to the shop, would you, Derek, we need some beans.'

Uncle Gobb snapped out of his standstill and scurried off to the shop.

Oh dear.

Malcolm knew, you know and I know that means …

… it means that Uncle Gobb will come back.

Oh no …

… and you know what Uncle Gobb coming back means?

It means that we'll meet him again.

But that'll have to be in another book.

Is this possible?

CHAPTER 34

Yes.

Yes, I think that can be arranged.

THE END!!!

INDEX

ACKNOWLEDGEMENTS

I would like to say thank you.

Disclaimer

All coincidences in this work are delicious.

Anyone living or dead is a book.

PROFILES

Michael Rosen grew up in 1946. He was born. He went on to become one of the … er … the … er… Later he was later. He lives in a place.

Neal Layton writes and draws, draws and writes, writes and draws, draws and writes. In his spare time, he spares time. His best is his best.

DEFINITIONS

Beans some beans in this book

Crackersnacker
a boy in this book

Dog a dog in this book

Infinity big

Pneumonoultramicroscopicsilicovolcanoconiosis
big word